www.tredition.de

AF202526

Monika Staudacher

SoulHeart

Stories for Heart and Soul

www.tredition.de

Publisher and printer:
tredition GmbH, Halenreie 40-44, 22359 Hamburg
Germany

ISBN
Paperback: 978-3-347-27403-7
Hardcover: 978-3-347-27404-4
e-Book: 978-3-347-27405-1

Thanks to all,

who have encouraged me

to believe in me.

My thanks also to the wonderful

Jaquie Lait,

herself an Inspirational Author,

for proofreading my translation

from German into English.

Chakras

Chakra, the Sanskrit word for "wheel," can be translated as energy center or vortex of power.

They are receivers and transformers for all energy vibrations and information that go beyond the physical realm, and thus are connecting gateways to our spiritual energy bodies and the cosmos.

Each chakra vibrates in its own frequency and color, and is responsible for the body, as well as spiritual-soul level.

The little soul

Once upon a time there was a little soul.

She lived together with her big family in the beautiful "place of free souls".

This was not a place as we know it here on earth, but rather a kind of huge cloud, filled with magnificent colors, love, happiness, fulfillment and peace. Here everything was connected harmonically, and together formed a great whole. Here there was no "must", but only simply "being".

One day the elders called upon the little soul and solemnly announced to it:

"Our dear little soul, you are now ready. We are sending you to earth on your very first mission to spread your medicine among the people to bring healing, hope, love and happiness to the world."

The little soul cheered, jumped, and danced for joy.

She had heard many stories from the old souls about the people, and this made her incredibly excited and curious.

On the day of her departure, the little soul said goodbye to her fellow souls. They all stood around her in a circle and gave her good advice for the journey she was about to embark on.

The elders handed her the backpack with the precious contents and helped her to strap it on.

"Good luck!"

"Take good care of yourself, and your medicine!"

"Hurry up so you can get there on time too!"

"Always stay true to yourself!"

"Don't forget our language!"

"Don't forget us!" the other souls shouted to her.

The little soul smiled. Of course, she would never forget her family and her wonderful soul home!

She turned around once more, waved, and then slid down the rainbow to the earth.

She really needed to hurry, because soon a little girl named Mara would be born, and she wanted to make sure that she arrived before the birth.

Gently and lovingly, the little soul slipped into the yet to be born body of little Mara and found a cozy place oh so very close to her wonderful, huge heart, that already beats in such a strong and beautiful rhythm.

It felt wonderful, so warm and soft.

As long as Mara lived, the little soul would be with her until the time came to return to her hometown.

Full of eagerness, the little soul set to work.

She took some medicine and lovingly rubbed Mara's heart with it. She put the rest back into her backpack.

Her medicine took effect immediately, and Mara's parents received their baby overjoyed and in great gratitude. From the first moment they felt an unconditional love for little Mara, and a warm smile spread over their faces and melted their hearts.

The little soul was very proud and satisfied with herself and her work.

***

In the course of time, she diligently gathered new experiences. She got to know and understand the world of people better, their way of thinking, feeling, acting and communicating with each other.

She found it strange that people listened more to their minds than to their hearts, but she tried hard to do the same.

She eagerly packed all the new knowledge into her backpack, which also contained her medicine at the bottom.

Very soon she had learned from the people how life really was, what one was allowed to think, feel, say and do, and what one was not allowed to do, how reality really was and what one only imagined.

She had learned that it was better to be suspicious and trust in fear, that it was important to keep one's possessions to oneself, and to secure one's heart so that no one could take it away.

Now she knew that it was better to stick to what you know, that life was not easy and carefree, that you had no automatic right to happiness and love, but instead had to work hard for it.

As time passed, however, the little soul somehow felt worse and sicker, and the weight of the backpack pulled heavily on her shoulders.

She gritted her teeth, worked even harder and gathered new knowledge even more diligently.

Her backpack was now so full that it was overflowing, and her new knowledge was already falling to the ground.

Little by little, the little soul's memories of the place she came from faded, and she lost the language of souls.

She became more and more sad, tired and powerless, without being able to explain it.

The family of souls watched the little soul anxiously. They wanted to help her and called out to her from the hometown, trying to tell her that she only had to look in her backpack at the bottom and find her medicine once again. Then she would be able to heal herself, shine with happiness again and remember who she was and why she had come to earth in the first place.

But it seemed that the words of the souls could no longer reach the little soul.

Sometimes the little soul thought she heard a gentle whisper, but she quickly pushed the thought aside. She knew now that such things could only be fantasies.

To help the little soul along, some of the older souls themselves slipped into bodies on earth.

They arranged encounters and certain situations, but the little soul no longer recognized her family.

Sometimes the little soul dreamed of a beautiful place that was strangely familiar. Actually, it was not a place at all, but rather a feeling of being and happiness, of familiarity, connectedness, unity and security. There it was peaceful and loving, quite different from here on earth. There were also no people, but ... hm, she could not really describe it ...

In these moments, an inexplicable, infinite longing filled the little soul.

***

The years and decades passed and the little soul still lived in Mara's body.

From the once happy and cheerful girl, became a grown woman who was occupied by her everyday life, and led, as society calls it, a normal life.

She didn't have a partner, but she REALLY wouldn't have had time for that. She often had to work overtime and was so tired in the evenings that she REALLY just wanted to lie on the sofa at home, watch a movie or read a book. She had to be REALLY happy to have a job at all, in which she earned enough money, she was not allowed to be REALLY picky. Life was not a concert of wishes. Even if it wasn't particularly exciting, she could still REALLY be quite content.

But why was there this feeling in her? This feeling, that there was still more, that there was something in her, slowly wasting away and just waiting to finally be freed.

***

The little soul sat huddled next to Mara's heart and looked at it sadly. She couldn't remember exactly what it was, but it seemed that it wasn't as warm, as bright, or as big as it had been in the beginning.

The little soul felt so weak and without energy that she mostly slept. She was so endlessly tired.

Once she gathered all her remaining strength and tried to stand up. But she didn't manage it, stumbled and hit the ground hard. The bulging backpack slipped off her thin shoulders, fell to the floor, burst open and the contents tumbled out.

Scattered there, now lay all the knowledge that the little soul had gathered since her first day on earth. All the beliefs, the new programs of the mind, the bad experiences, the narcissistic ego and ... there was something else that somehow seemed familiar to her.

The little soul took it in her hand, turned it back and forth and with one blow the memory came back with full force.

It was her medicine!

A feeling of happiness flowed through her.

She remembered ... everything ... her soul-family, her hometown and her mission here on earth!

How could she have forgotten all of that?

With a sudden feeling of relief, she realised that the heavy burden had disappeared from her shoulders and she felt fresh energy flowing into her again.

She immediately felt much better and happier and now she knew once again what to do.

The little soul went to Mara's grey heart, held it lovingly, gently spread a little medicine on it and whispered something to it.

***

Mara was on her lunch break.

She was sitting outside on a bench in the park, listlessly biting into her sandwich.

Lately she had not been feeling very well. She was often irritable, constantly tired and somehow she didn't really enjoy anything anymore. Her friends had already talked to her about it, but she didn't know what was wrong with her. Maybe she should go to the doctor and have her blood values checked.

Just as she was lost in her thoughts, she felt a strange tingling in her chest and her heart began to beat wildly.

She became a bit frightened and searched the park with her eyes for a possible emergency responder.

She was surprised to see that the leaves were already growing on the trees and that the sky was bright blue.

She had not noticed that before. Hmmm..., it smelled like fresh grass and flowers!

Deeply she inhaled the fresh air and her heartbeat calmed down.

How strange ...

Quite unexpectedly, a childlike joy rose up in her and she had the urgent need to jump and dance right there and now, no matter what others might think of her.

Her tiredness was swept away, giving way to new energy and drive.

Thoughts circled in her head.

Why was she even sitting around here?

Why did she go to this musty office every day and do things she didn't really enjoy?

What had happened to the fun-loving, curious, adventurous Mara and her big dreams?

It was as if she heard a very quiet voice inside her, a voice that seemed to come from her heart, encouraging her.

A thought germinated in her, grew bigger and spread more and more.

In one fell swoop, she was clearer than she had ever been in her life.

Determined, she got up, grabbed her purse, and threw the rest of the tasteless sandwich into the trash can.

She would talk to her boss right now and quit.

She wasn't going to settle for "it'll be fine" anymore.

No, she wanted more!

She wanted her "superduperbestofall" life and to finally do what she really, really loved and what she found fulfilling.

She wanted to be happy because she deserved it, no, because she was WORTH it!

Joyfully excited, she set off eagerly into her new life to live her heart's mission and spread her very unique "medicine" to the world.

Wave and spiral

See the constant up and down, the end and the new beginning.

Each of your decisions has an effect on yourself and on your environment.

In sum, your decisions describe the spiral of your life.

Decision

Pale as a sheet, Nikas Rathenburg hung up the phone.

Once again, his parents had simply decided something for him without asking what he actually wanted.

He clenched his fists in annoyance.

***

The name Nikas (without an "l"!) meant as much as "the winner".

What irony, because he did not feel like that at all! Rather, he felt very lonely.

He was an only child.

For as long as he could remember, his parents had been busy making the company empire even bigger, even better, even more profitable, even more powerful. There was not much time left for him. He was also unable to build up a real relationship with the constantly changing nannies who took care of him.

The Rathenburgs' estate still sent a shiver down Nikas' spine.

He had never felt it to be a place of love and security, a refuge, or his home.

When he was eleven, his parents sent him to an elite international boarding school in London.

Although the children there were allowed to go home every other weekend, his parents usually only had him picked up for a few days during the semester break.

So Nikas spent most of his time at the boarding school during his entire school and university years.

He passed the time by studying, playing sports and reading, and was soon the best in his class at everything.

He had no friends. His classmates teased him for being a nerd, and most of the kids only stayed at the boarding school for a short time anyway.

But he did have one friend.

It was John, the janitor.

John liked the bright, intelligent boy who always tried to live up to everyone's expectations.

He sensed how lonely Nikas was, so he often asked him to help with chores at the boarding school on weekends.

John taught Nikas how to change lamps, clean drains, paint walls, mow the lawn, prune the roses, and anything else that needed doing.

Nikas' favorite place to be with John was in the small workshop. There they repaired the most diverse devices and machines and sometimes even built small pieces of furniture. It turned out that he had a great creative talent and manual skills.

After work, John took Nikas to his home, where his wife Nina usually prepared a delicious meal.

The three of them would sit in the kitchen in front of the open fireplace, where a warm fire always burned in the winter, and talk about God and the world.

Nikas loved being with the two of them, laughing and ... yes, just being happy.

He could confide everything to them, including his fears, wishes and dreams. With them, he could just be who he was. THAT felt for him like his home.

***

John and Nina also enjoyed having Nikas around.

They could not have children of their own and loved Nikas like their own son.

So quickly the years of study had passed! He had a nice room here on campus and actually felt quite comfortable.

A few days ago, Nikas was sitting in the kitchen again with John and Nina. They were eating, having a glass of wine, laughing, and Nikas was telling them about the many plans he had made for his life after college.

First of all, he wanted to take a year off, travel and explore the world. He wanted to have adventures, try new things, and gain lots of experiences to find out who he really was, what he was really passionate about, and how he wanted to shape his future. He wanted a fulfilled life and later a woman at his side whom he loved, and with whom he also wanted to start a family.

Tomorrow was now going to be the day.

The long-awaited day of graduation was approaching and he was already a bit excited.

The phone call he received from his mother a few minutes ago had upset him greatly. She wanted to make sure that he had already reserved good seats in the front row for the celebration.

Since his relationship with his parents was rather cool and formal, it surprised him that his mother sounded strangely nervous and childishly joyful. After pushing around a bit, she told him the big secret his father was going to tell him tomorrow.

He had bought a new company, which he wanted to give to Nikas for the successful completion of his studies.

Nikas was also to then take over its management with immediate effect and be registered as an equal partner in the company empire.

Everything was already prepared and the appointment with the notary was arranged for the afternoon after graduation.

Speechless and as white as a sheet, Nikas had hung up the phone ...

***

Oh no!!! That was not HIS plan! At least not yet! He had to explore the world first and find out WHAT HE really wanted!

Desperately, he grabbed his jacket and ran down into the town to the pub.

He didn't remember how many glasses of ale he had drunk that night, and he had no idea when and how he had gotten home, but in any case, he had a pretty heavy buzz ...

***

Exhausted and tired, Nikas unlockes the door of his villa and steps into the large foyer.

Everything is quiet. No one is running toward him. No one is waiting for him.

He put the key with his company's silver logo in the noble wooden bowl on the dresser and throws his Armani jacket over the antique arm-chair. He slips the Italian designer shoes off his feet and picks up the stack of mail that the maid has already laid out for him.

The top letter is from some business institute.

Recipient: "Dr. Niklas Rathenburg ..."

He sighs. Another person who didn't spell his first name right! No wonder! It was so typical of his parents that they had chosen this name for him! Nikas, the winner! It was always about winning, power, success and money!

Sure, he was indeed one of the most successful entrepreneurs in the world, making huge profits every year and flying all over the world. He had a beautiful villa on the outskirts of the city with an unobstructed view of the countryside, and his garage was home to a considerable collection of expensive cars.

But did that make him a winner?

He felt so lonely.

Although he was extremely attractive, he was not married. He didn't even have a steady girl-friend. Of course, there were women in his life, even many, pretty, young women who were just waiting to grab the eligible bachelor. But he did-n't really love any of them and had the feeling that the ladies were more interested in his fortune than in him.

He presses the answering machine button and listens to his mother's message:

"Hello Nikas. You're thinking about dinner Saturday night? We're expecting you at 7:00. Oh yes, happy birthday from me and your father. I hope your secretary gave you the bottle of cognac from us. So, we'll see you tomorrow. Please be on time."

He rolled his eyes.

Why was she calling about this?

They were expecting him for dinner EVERY Saturday night.

This was not an invitation where he had a choice, no, it was a compulsory event where there was no escape.

These evenings always went the same way.

First, he greeted his mother with a stiff kiss on the cheek and then met his father in the fireplace room with a glass of cognac.

His father asked him to report on the development of business and the figures for the past week, until they were fetched by the maid for dinner in the large salon.

There, the three of them sat at the huge, dark wooden table.

Mostly, his mother steered the conversation to some young daughter of a rich, friendly business partner who would be a good match for him.

Either Nikas set an alarm and pretended it was an urgent phone call, or he came up with some other excuse to leave his parents' estate as soon as possible.

Wearing socks, Nikas walks across the dark wooden floor into the sterile, cool stainless steel kitchen. His housekeeper always put a plate of food in the refrigerator for him to warm up. While he heats up his meal in the microwave, he pours himself a glass of martini.

Except for the bottle of expensive cognac that was sitting on his desk in his office this morning, along with a simple birthday card from his parents, it had been a normal day, like almost every day he had spent in recent years.

He made one phone call after another, rushed from meeting to meeting, met for a quick lunch with a foreign partner, had to make some unpleasant and far-reaching decisions, and yet in the evening had the feeling of having accomplished nothing.

Sometimes he felt like a hamster in a wheel. The faster he ran, the faster the wheel turned.

His family doctor had been warning him for years that he needed to get more rest. But that was easier said than done.

Plate and mail in hand, he saunters into the living room. He turns on the CNN news channel on the huge plasma screen, sits down on the dark tan leather sofa, pokes listlessly at his food, flipping through the letters.

Bill, bill, ad, bill, ...

What was that?! ... His name and address are neatly handwritten on a dark blue envelope. On the back is the return address: John and Nina Walker.

Joy spreads through him and, at the same time, his guilty conscience.

Hastily, he tears open the letter. A card, a small candle and an old photo fall out of the envelope.

The photo shows little Nikas on his tenth birthday. He proudly holds up his gift, a red Swiss army knife, and stands in front of the cake with the ten burning candles, his eyes shining and his cheeks puffed out.

Nikas opens the card.

A paper cake pops up and a distorted "Happy Birthday Song" plays.

"Dear Nikas,

we wish you all the best and love on your birthday from the bottom of our hearts. We think of you often and hope you are living exactly the life you always wanted. I recently found this photo in a box. We remember John showing you how to carve a pipe with your pocket knife. You were so proud of it! Maybe you are married now and have children of your own that you can teach to carve. We would be so happy to see you again.

John is a little dizzy sometimes and the doctor says to take it easy, but you know John, he doesn't want to know about it. Other than that, we're doing great. Feel tightly squeezed!

Yours, Nina and John."

Tears run down the cheeks of the tall, grown-up, successful and infinitely lonely Nikas.

He rummages in the drawer of the living room table for the Swiss Army knife, takes it in his hand and looks at it.

Today was his thirty-fifth birthday ... how he would have loved to celebrate it with John and Nina.

Every year he received a letter from them on his birthday!

And him? He hadn't contacted them in such a long time. Actually, he wanted to visit them, but somehow he always lacked the time.

He admitted to himself that he was also afraid of it.

He was ashamed of his life, which was no fun for him, because it really only consisted of work and he had no time and energy for other things.

How could he explain to them that he had betrayed himself and his dreams, that he hadn't discovered the world, had adventures, and hadn't discovered his true calling?

Sobbing, he curles up on the sofa and cries for all of his unlived dreams.

***

... somewhere it rings...

***

It takes Nikas quite a while to realize that it's the alarm clock on his cell phone.

What the hell ...?

He is drenched in sweat, a pale taste fills his mouth and his head threatens to burst at the slightest movement.

Slowly, he opens his eyes and blinks into the sunlight shining through the window.

He is lying in his bed in his dorm room, dressed ...

The screen of his cell phone tells him it's 9:30.
A reminder pops up: 11 a.m. graduation day today!

Confused, Nikas remains lying there for a moment. His thoughts race through his brain as if they were playing tag.

Why Graduation Day? What was going on with his company, his villa, ...?

Gradually, his thoughts return to reality.

"Thank God! So, it's not too late!" he sighs in relief. "It was just a dream!"

Ignoring the stabbing hangover pain in his head, he flips back the covers and stands up.

He dissolves an aspirin in water and empties the entire glass in one go.

The cold water of the refreshing shower washes away the last veils and doubts from him.

He carefully combs his hair, pulls on his white shirt and slips into the silver-grey suit his parents sent him for today's graduation ceremony.

As he ties his burgundy tie, he winks conspiratorially at his reflection in the mirror.

He has made a decision.

He goes to the closet, fishes the large touring backpack from the top shelf and puts a few things on the bed.

Hiking boots, sneakers, a bit of clothing, washing kit, passport, cell phone, wallet, sunglasses and the red Swiss Army knife.

Everything is ready ...

HE is ready ...

A pleasant feeling of happiness, mixed with exciting excitement and a sense of adventure, flows through him.

He takes a deep breath, grabs his black robe and beret, and heads off to his graduation celebration and his new, exciting life.

Yes!

He is Nikas!

He is a winner!

Butterfly

How wonderful is the transformation of a caterpillar into a butterfly.

A new beginning in a different form, a further development of abilities and the completion of growth.

A symbol of transformation, rebirth and the soul.

Embrace

The air smells of spring and the birds are chirping in joyful anticipation. The fresh green leaves of the trees catch the sun's rays and bees fly busily among the first daffodils and tulips.

Jessica sits on the bench on which she has already sat so many countless times and looks blankly at the small lake in front of her. Salty traces of dried tears cover her cheeks.

A few ducks swim in the pond, but Jessica takes no notice. For her it is a colorless, mute and joyless day, like all days since the ONE.

Why?

Why couldn't she stop it?

Why was she so powerless?

How could she go on living like this?

***

Six years ago, Jessica was also sitting on that bench crying. Her grandmother had died, and she thought of all the beautiful memories from her childhood. How her grandma used to send her down a basket of sweets from the second floor on a long rope when she was playing in the garden.

She could still clearly remember the taste of the chocolate candies covered with pink and white peppermint icing. She loved her grandma very much and now she just wasn't there anymore.

Suddenly, music mingled with her grief.

Apparently, someone nearby was playing the guitar and singing along. What a voice! So beautiful!

Jessica was curious, sighed, stood up, and then, as if magically attracted, walked in the direction from which the sounds were coming.

After a few minutes she came across the source of these beautiful sounds.

She saw a young man who, with his eyes closed, was completely devoted to his playing and singing.

She examined him closely.

His blond hair stood out tousled in surfer style from his head. He wore washed-out jeans that slipped a bit below his hips, revealing the lettering "Calvin Klein." The black T-shirt with the inscription "Hard Rock Café" lay tightly over his muscular belly and the long, somewhat shabby-looking, leather coat gave him a certain cowboy look. Even the white, worn sneakers had their best days behind them.

He looked incredibly good!!!

In the open guitar case, which was covered with stickers from all over the world, there were already quite a few coins.

When the song was over, the young man opened his stunning blue eyes and looked directly into those of Jessica.

The surrounding audience applauded enthusiastically, threw a few more coins into the guitar case and then went their separate ways.

The young man smiled mischievously and looked bluntly at Jessica, who was still standing rooted to the spot.

Then he walked up to her, took her head between his hands and kissed her unexpectedly right on the mouth.

Blood rushed to Jessica's head, her cheeks glowed, and her body trembled.

What did he think he was doing?

Who did he think he was?

Annoyed, she tried to ignore the joyful leap of her heart.

The young man grinned up to both ears, pointed at the coins he had just earned and asked,"Hey, I'm Luke. You up for some coffee? Come on, my treat!"

Without waiting for her response, he gathered his things, took her hand, and pulled her with him through the park to a small coffee shop.

Jessica, still feeling his lips on hers, slowly regained consciousness.

Luke was bursting with joie de vivre, exuberance, and positive energy, so she could no longer stay mad at him.

They sat down at a small table and ordered two cappuccinos.

She enjoyed being in his company and being infected by his lightness and cheerfulness.

They talked and laughed until the waitress informed them that the café would now like to close.

Luke told her that he was leaving early the next morning. He did not have a fixed destination yet, because he loved to just drift and be surprised where it led him.

Jessica didn't want to say goodbye to Luke yet. She felt that she had fallen in love with him, this had never happened to her before.

Since he didn't have a place to stay for the night, Jessica offered him her sofa. She had never done anything like that before either!

They drank a few glasses of wine on the balcony by candlelight and each of them could feel that special crackle that existed between them ...

The next morning Jessica woke up with a smile. Wow! What a passionate night of love!

She felt next to her, but the sheet was cold and Luke was not there.

She looked over at the untouched sofa and discovered a small note on it with the words:

"Dear Jessica,

I didn't want to wake you up because I left early. Thank you for the beautiful day and the amazing night with you. I have never experienced anything like this before and I am not just saying that now. You are very special.

Maybe I'll write a song about it someday. I hope our paths cross again someday. I will never forget you.

From the bottom of my heart

Luke."

She felt a twinge in her heart. How she wished he had stayed with her. She didn't even know his last name ...

***

Almost four months after that very special night, Jessica gently stroked her belly and lovingly looked at the first ultrasound image of her baby.

She had just found out she was pregnant, and a thousand thoughts were racing through her mind.

She couldn't quite believe it yet, but one thing was very clear to her:

She would have this baby of love and passion. It would probably never meet its father, but she would tell him how wonderful he was and how much she was in love with him.

And she would love this baby more than anything else in the world!

***

On a clear day in January, little Henry was born.

He was a real sunshine, had the same tousled hair as his father, the same bright blue eyes and the same dazzling smile.

And ...

he had an aggressive tumor in his brain that could not be treated ...

***

At the thought of her son, Jessica smiles sadly and continues to stare blankly at the lake. She doesn't even notice the beautiful, shimmering golden butterfly that is fluttering around the bench all the time.

***

Jessica often took Henry for walks in the park and every time they sat down together on this bench and watched the ducks on the lake.

On one of those days, Henry was about two years old, something very strange happened.

With his head down and his shoulders slumped, an old man walked past them. His steps seemed to be difficult for him.

Then Henry climbed down from the bench, ran up to him, looked up at him, smiled at him and hugged him. Better said, he hugged the old man's legs, because he was still so small.

"Well, little one, you're cute," the old man murmured, smiling in wonder and stroking Henry's head affectionately.

This moment had something so deep, powerful, intimate, honest and ... somehow magical about it.

Henry released the embrace, waved goodbye to the old man and climbed back onto the park bench to join his mother as if it were the most natural thing in the world.

The man lifted his hat in salute, nodded to them both with a smile, and walked away again.

His steps seemed lighter now, his body was more upright, and his gaze wandered to the beautiful nature around him.

When Jessica asked Henry why he had done that, Henry tilted his head, gave her his bright smile, shrugged his shoulders and said, "Old Grandpa so sad, Eny ouch away." Then he snuggled up to his mommy and dozed off for a bit.

Since that day, Henry was always hugging strangers.

He had an unerring sense for when someone was sad, lonely, or sick, or when someone just wasn't feeling well.

Sometimes people were just surprised, but most of the time they were very touched.

In the end, however, there was always a gentle, happy smile on everyone's face and they seemed to somehow radiate from within.

***

Jessica's eyes fill with tears again.

Shortly before Henry's sixth birthday, the doctors diagnosed that it would probably be the last one Henry would experience.

To the end, however, Henry insisted on going to the park with Jessica.

At one point he asked her, "Mom, why are so many people so sad and alone? All they need is a little love!"

Jessica hugged him lovingly and he wrapped his thin little arms around her.

"Mom, you don't have to be sad either! I may be going back soon, but I'll always love you!"

***

Her eyes filled with tears again.

What a smart, brave and wonderful boy he had been.

And there it was again, that deep, almost unbearable pain of memory that pierced her heart like a dagger every time.

Sobbing, she hid her face in her hands and gave in to the next crying attack.

Why him?

Why him?

Why now?

He was still so young!!!

What was she supposed to do?

How was she supposed to get through this?

This sadness, loneliness and senselessness was more than she could bear.

Then she feels a comforting hand on her shoulder.

With teary eyes she looks into the familiar face of the old man, who smiles at her full of compassion.

Next to him are many other people, all familiar faces, all people to whom Henry had once given comfort and new courage with his embraces.

Now they are hugging Jessica, giving her a warm smile and comforting words.

"We are so sorry. Your little son was there for us when things were bad. He gave us back hope and brought new happiness and joy into our lives. He healed our soul wounds and for that we are infinitely grateful to him and to you as well. Please let us know if there is anything, we can do for you. We will never forget our Henry. He was a little angel."

They pat Jessica's shoulders again and squeeze her hand as a sign of their sympathy and say goodbye with the words, "You can be very proud of him."

Jessica feels deep gratitude, connection and love mingling with her grief, and her heart knows that someday the pain will get a little easier. It would certainly be a long road ahead, but the healing had already begun.

At that moment, she hears beautiful guitar music and a chant that is somehow familiar and touches her heart ...

An incredulous, joyful smile flits across Jessica's face, bringing back a bit of color and life to her.

With slightly flushed cheeks, she stands up and walks with quick steps in the direction from which the music seems to come.

***

The shimmering golden butterfly settles down on the park bench.

Satisfied, it slowly opens and closes its wings and shows itself in all its beauty.

White feather

When you see a white feather,

you may remember

that your guardian angel is always with you

and taking care of you.

Seeing with the heart

Seventeen-year-old Kevin stood in the doorway of the kitchen with a frown on his face and his arms folded in a pout.

His mother was busy preparing dinner and he heard her putting plates and silverware on the table.

He smelled that his favorite meal, barbecue chicken and chips, was being served.

"Now don't be like that, Kevin!" His mother nudged him encouragingly on the shoulder. "I'm sure it will be totally nice and fun!"

Kevin disagreed completely, though.

He had absolutely no desire to spend the summer at a nature camp with this weird youth group he didn't know at all.

He hated the feeling of helplessness when he was somewhere he didn't know.

He hated being with strangers.

He hated being pitied, and he hated it even more when people pretended that everything was normal and that they did not pity him.

In short, he hated going to that camp.

For as long as he could remember, Kevin had always spent summer vacations with his parents and his sister Maia in a French cottage in Brittany.

He loved the small French village, the narrow, cool streets, the shrieking of children playing, the salty smell of the air, the sound of the sea and the fresh wind that ran through his dark, curly hair.

Most people there knew him from an early age and didn't ask him any questions. Everything was familiar to him there, so he felt safe and secure.

"But why can't we go to Brittany like we do every year?" he asked irritably.

"Oh honey, we've talked about this so many times. Your father doesn't have time this year because he has an important project to finish, and I have to fill in for my colleague because she's in the hospital," his mother replied patiently. Maia is going to Italy with her friend's family and this camp is a nice change for you. You'll experience something new and meet other young people who are also in the same situation..."

She didn't finish the sentence, but Kevin knew what she wanted to say.

Young people who were also like him, who were also different from others, who were also "handicapped", as they said, so as not to have to use the word "handicapped".

But that's what he was, handicapped!

When he was three years old, he was diagnosed with a rare eye disease. The doctors tried everything in their power, but in the end, they could not prevent him from eventually going blind.

His world consisted only of rough, greyish shadows. Grey, lighter grey, darker grey, but always this grey, grey-full grey!

In the meantime, his family was able to cope with the situation quite well and Kevin, too, had of course learned at the school for the blind to get along as well as possible in his everyday life.

But he was so angry!

So angry at everything and everyone, even though he knew that no one was to blame for his illness.

And still!

And he simply didn't feel like going to this stupid camp, where there were all kinds of different disabled people.

Basta!

"Everything is really well organized and to-morrow you will be picked up directly from here at home. You'll all go to the camp together by bus. Isn't that great? I'm so happy for you! It's going to be so exciting!" His mother gave him an unexpected kiss on the cheek.

***

Serena was sitting at the kitchen table.

In front of her was the brochure of the youth camp, which she had already read through countless times.

She was so excited. Her suitcase had been packed and ready in the hallway for days.

Serena knew how hard it was for her single mother to manage everything. The work at the clinic, the household and then her too.

They didn't have much money, and her mother had been saving for a long time for Serena to go to this camp.

It was the first time in her life that Serena traveled alone, the first time without her mom.

She was so happy to experience something new, to meet other young people and to spend a lot of time in nature and fresh air.

She loved nature!

Sometimes, when her mom had a day off, they would go to the park with the little lake where lots of ducks were swimming.

She would sit in her wheelchair on the shore and throw the ducks little pieces of hard bread.

She smiled at the thought.

"What are you thinking about right now, sweetheart? It must be something very nice, because you've been grinning to yourself all along."

Serena's mother stepped behind her and gently placed her hands on Serena's shoulders.

"Oh, mama! I'm just so happy! I'm so looking forward to camp and the other youngsters, and I'm already so excited, I can hardly wait until tomorrow!"

Gratefully, she looked up at her mom.

"Thank you mom. Thank you for doing this for me. Love you so much!"

Serena threw her mom a flying kiss.

Touched, Serena's mom hugged her daughter.

"I wish I could do so much more for you, sweetheart. I'm so proud of you for the way you're handling it all and what a wonderful young woman you've become. Love you too!" She pressed a big peck on Serena's cheek.

***

At eleven o'clock sharp in the morning, the bus arrived.

Kevin had his dark sunglasses on and was already waiting outside the front door with his mother.

"Wait a minute! I'll help you!" offered Kevin's mother, wanting to take the suitcase.

"No!" exclaimed Kevin annoyed, turning around to grab the suitcase and tripping over it.

Angry and cursing, he scrambled back up and fumbled again for the suitcase.

He felt the light pressure of his mother's warm, gentle hand on his arm as she pulled him close and gave him a quick goodbye hug.

"I wish you a lot of fun, my darling. You'll see, everything will be fine!"

Hesitantly, he returned the hug, nodded once more to his mother, and then ran toward the sound of the engine.

The driver took his luggage from him, stowed it, and led him to his seat on the bus.

"This is Kevin," he said tersely, then got back behind his wheel and drove off.

Okay. So now he was on this goddamn bus that would take him to this goddamn camp, along with these goddamn other cripples.

Just as he was about to demonstratively put on his thick headphones and fully indulge in his murky thoughts, a SOMEWHAT tapped his shoulders.

"Hi Kevin, I'm Serena. It's nice to meet you. I was the first one picked up, so I was able to snag this seat up front. Earlier, another boy wanted to sit next to me, but the bus driver said it was already reserved for you. So, I was already curious about you. You know, I'm really looking forward to the camp because I've never done anything like this before. I've never been away alone. Well, it's not alone, but I mean without my mom, so just like that, with others. That is so exciting! I'm really excited about what we're going to do! I don't know anyone yet, but I'm sure we'll be a really nice group. There are as many girls as boys, which is really cool! I turned sixteen this year..."

OH MY GOD!!! How could someone blabber on so much in one piece!!!?

Kevin's head almost seemed to burst. This was getting off to a good start. That was all he needed.

He just wanted to have his peace, nothing else.

He would have to serve his time in the camp, but he would certainly not have any fun.

He put on his headphones, crossed his arms in front of his chest, and demonstratively turned his body away from the nonsense bus.

The bus kept stopping to pick up other passengers, and at some point, Kevin even managed to doze off a bit.

After a few hours of driving, he was awakened by a rattling and shaking.

The rattling came from the bus, which seemed to be struggling with some pretty uneven ground, the shaking came from his talkative neighbor, who tugged him by the sleeve.

"Hey Kevin, wake up! We'll be right there! You've got to come see this! You can already see the cabins back there! Can you see them?"

"No, I can't," Kevin replied curtly.

"Well there, between the trees! You must see that!"

"But I don't!" yelled Kevin at Serena. "Because I'm blind! But you probably didn't notice that because you were talking so much!"

"Oh...! I'm ... sorry about that! Sorry not that you're blind, well yes, of course you are, but I mean that I didn't notice. Really sorry! How stupid of me! I was just so excited and looking forward to camp. I'm really sorry!", Serena apologized sincerely.

"It's okay," Kevin muttered.

"You know what? I'm going to make it up to you. From so-forth, I'll be your eyes here at camp, and I'll describe everything I see to you in great detail. I promise!"

Oh great! Now that's what he got! A personal "guide dog" in the form of a talkative sixteen-year-old!

When the bus pulled up to the large plaza in front of the camp, they were already greeted by the counselors and given a warm welcome.

They gathered in the common room, where they formed a circle of chairs.

One after the other they had to introduce themselves and tell a little bit about themselves.

What a group they were!

They were four girls and four boys.

There was:

Him, Kevin, the blind one;

Serena, who was in a wheelchair because her legs were paralyzed;

Jonny, who was born with only one arm;

Bill, who had to run around all day wearing a helmet because sometimes he would just suddenly lose consciousness and fall down;

Marie, who had Down Syndrome;

Sally, who spoke so softly because of a traumatic experience that she could hardly be understood;

Michi, who suffered from severe neurodermatitis and always wore gloves because otherwise he would scratch himself bloody,

and Alice, who was suffering from leukemia and as a result of chemo therapy had no hair anymore.

The four caregivers also introduced themselves. They were two men and two women, all between twenty-five and thirty years old. They were very nice and explained what they were going to do with the young people over the next few days.

The program included various games in nature, swimming in the lake, a few small excursions, various creative workshops, cooking together and in the evening a campfire with guitar music.

After a delicious, simple dinner, they were dismissed to the two four-bed rooms and helped to get along with everything. Everyone was given a flashlight and an emergency beeper for the night and then they all fell asleep very quickly, exhausted from the trip and all the excitement.

The next day, a scavenger hunt was planned. It was not about speed, but about discovering a total of ten places as a team, each with a riddle to solve.

Each team consisted of a boy and a girl who had to work together and support each other.

It was clear that Serena was Kevin's buddy, because she had arranged it that way.

Although Kevin had planned to be pissed off and just get the time at camp over with as quickly as possible, he enjoyed the change, the different sounds and smells of the forest, and the fresh air. He was starting to get used to the camp and the company of the other "cripples"and was even kind of happy that Serena was his buddy.

She was so bubbly, happy and lively that it rubbed off a little on him too.

The other three teams consisted of Down-Syndrom-Marie and Helmet-Bill; Whisper-Sally and Jonny-one-arm, and Alice-without-hair along with Glove-Michi.

Each team was given a starting puzzle, a backpack with two water bottles, snacks, a thin blanket, a map of the area around the camp, and binoculars.

In addition, everyone was to put on their emergency beeper.

And then it went off. Each team strayed off in a different direction.

Serena read the first riddle to Kevin:

"Go to where the sun rises from its bed and visit the five giants who have gathered for council. There, where they shelter, you will find the next riddle. Hmmm..."

"Then it must be east!" exclaimed Kevin.

"Yes, exactly!!! The sun rises in the east! So, all we have to do is go in the right direction and find five giants!" rejoiced Serena.

"What could possibly be meant by giants? Maybe five rocks, or something. In any case, there has to be five big things that you can see clearly and that somehow belong together," Kevin reasoned.

"Well, we'll figure that out! Now chop-chop!!! Let's just get going or it will get dark before we even get started," laughed Serena.

They quickly found the direction where the sun had risen in the morning and Kevin tried to push Serena's wheelchair over the uneven gravel path.

However, the stones and depressions made it an extremely strenuous and bumpy endeavour.

"I have an idea!" exclaimed Serena.

"Let's just leave the wheelchair here. You could carry me on your shoulders, and I'll tell you where to go. We'll move a lot faster that way! I'm not particularly heavy, and you're big and strong (and good-looking, Serena thought to herself as she walked). What do you think?"

Kevin liked the idea.

He was a little excited because he had never had such close physical contact with a strange girl before.

He knelt in front of Serena's rolling chair, she lifted her legs over his shoulders and held onto his head while he stood up.

She was light as a feather and her body felt so familiar.

A warm feeling flowed through Kevin.

Because of his blindness, his other senses were very strong and he perceived things that other people did not register so consciously.

Normally, he could even hear the beating of hearts as he walked past someone.

Oddly enough, he couldn't hear Serena's heartbeat ... how strange!

"Am I not too heavy for you either?" asked Serena cautiously.

"No, not at all! I can hardly feel you!", Kevin replied, and again that strange tingling ran through him.

"Okay! You're already standing just right. The path is a little rocky, but there's no big obstacle ahead or anything. So, you can just go ahead."

She patted her thighs and clicked her tongue as if trying to spur a horse.

As Kevin got moving, enjoying the slight swaying weight on his shoulders, Serena described to him everything she saw, "We're walking on a light-colored gravel path that goes through a forest. The path is a bit curved and in pretty good shape, so no big holes or anything. There are a lot of tall spruce trees here, with the sun's rays shining through them. Green, fresh moss grows on the ground, and you'd love to just fall into it. On the moss there are small and big branches, brown needles and cones from the spruces everywhere. And when the sun shines through the trees onto the fern leaves, sometimes a few drops of water glisten. It is so beautiful here! There are also a few wild strawberries growing on the edge here, but no sign of any five giants yet. The sky is light blue with a few white clouds in it. One of them looks like a small rabbit. It's getting a little lighter up ahead. I think that's where the forest ends."

Kevin liked the way Serena described the surroundings.

No one had ever done it that way for him before.

He could picture it clearly, and he could almost feel the soft moss she was talking about.

"Uiiiii!!!! Deer!!! They jump across the path right in front of us into a little clearing! How cute! And standing there ... Oh...!"

"What is it? What do you see? Tell me!", Kevin prompted Serena.

"Ha! I think we've found our five giants! There are five trees in a circle in the clearing. They almost look like us in our circle of chairs. What do you think? Could the trees mean giants?" asked Serena excitedly.

"We'll know in a minute. Come on, let's go!" replied Kevin.

"This is really fun! Wait, turn ninety degrees to the right. Good. Now take a really big step forward with your left leg. You have to step over a little ditch that runs right in front of you. Great! That's it! Now just straight ahead, right through the tall grass. I think I'll have to check you for ticks there later!"

She laughed.

"Okay. Stop! We're here! Hmmm ... what was it called? Where they shelter .... Let's walk around each tree. If you extend your right arm to the right, you can touch the first tree. It has white bark and leaves!"

"Then it's probably a birch tree," Kevin opined.

He carefully felt the tree, feeling the rough bark under his fingers, some of which was covered with lichen. An earthy, strong smell rose to his nose. Deeply he sucked in the air. How beautiful it was!

"So, I can't discover anything! Where then do the trees provide shelter? In the branches? Under the leaves? Maybe a nest in the tree? But we'll never get there!" thought Serena aloud.

"No, I don't think so. That would be way too dangerous! Maybe we'll find something on the ground by the roots. Some kind of cave or something," Kevin reasoned.

They examined each tree closely until they actually discovered something in the last one. Under a root was a hollow space, which could be a refuge for small animals. And inside was actually the note for the next riddle.

Serena and Kevin were really in their element and solved one riddle after the other.

They were a really good team, having fun and laughing a lot.

Kevin carried Serena on his shoulders and Serena described the world to Kevin as she saw it, dazzling, colorful, happy and just beautiful.

Her descriptions were so vivid that Kevin almost thought he was seeing it all himself.

At the same time, he wondered if he could even perceive the world with his own eyes anywhere near as intensely as Serena did for him.

He felt better than he had in a long time, so full of energy and drive, so alive, so ... happy.

Serena also enjoyed sitting on Kevin's shoulders.

In this way, it was almost as if she herself was walking through the tall grass, over ditches and along uneven paths.

She loved sharing her impressions with Kevin, describing everything to him in detail, and thus feeling it much more strongly herself.

She was even more cheerful than usual and felt somehow ... yes, ... whole.

She would miss no longer being carried by this strong, initially somewhat grumpy, but incredibly handsome young man, through whom she was allowed to experience a piece of freedom.

On the way back, they had enough time to take a long break on a bench by the stream.

Kevin carefully set Serena down.

Only now did they realize how hungry they actually were, so they unpacked their sandwiches and water bottles under the big old willow tree and told each other their stories.

Kevin described how he had started out as a normal, happy toddler who loved to romp around and create his own fantasy worlds with the big, colorful Lego bricks. He described how, over time, the building blocks became more and more blurred and colorless before his eyes.

Hopes faded more and more after each visit to the doctor and each further examination, until finally his whole world turned into a gray desert. He confided in Serena how powerless, lonely, angry and useless he often felt, and that he had no idea what his future might be as a blind adult.

It amazed him himself that he was so open and honest with her. He hadn't even been that to himself before.

Serena listened to Kevin sadly. She could understand so well how it felt when one's world changed from one moment to the next.

She told Kevin about her passion, dancing, and about the day her father had wanted to drive her to ballet class because it was raining so hard.

A few tears ran down her cheek as she came to the place where she had woken up in the hospital. Her mother had been sitting next to her bed, stroking her hand, her eyes red from all the tears she must have shed in the days before.

Serena had not remembered anything, only two glaring headlights, and she had guessed that something terrible must have happened. She had tried to push the blanket away with her legs, but nothing had moved.

Her father ..., she swallowed, ... had died at the scene of the accident and the doctors said it was a great miracle that Serena had survived.

Kevin felt her tender body shaking and put his arm around her comfortingly.

Serena calmed down a bit and went on to talk about how grateful she was to still be alive and to have her mom, despite everything.

"Thank goodness it's only my legs! I can't dance like I used to, but I play the piano and with my wheelchair I'm quite mobile. When I finish school, I want to study art and music and maybe become a teacher, I'd love that!"

Kevin admired Serena.

How could she still be so positive after all that had happened to her?

As they sat there talking, Kevin was overcome by a very strange "all is well" feeling, a sense of warmth, security, and ... yes, something else new that he had not yet experienced in that form.

Serena felt Kevin's comforting arm around her and emotions stirred within her as well.

What an extraordinary young man Kevin was.

His rough shell, with which he tried to protect his inner vulnerability, had cracked her from the beginning, because it was her gift to be able to look into the hearts and souls of people.

And in Kevin there was something very big, he just didn't know it yet, because it was still buried under some layers of anger, rage, fear and sadness.

But now SHE was there, and she would make sure that he recognized this greatness.

Sooner or later, he would understand.

Understand that losing his sight was just the gift he needed to REALLY SEE and help people.

The days at camp flew by.

Kevin never thought he would have so much fun here.

But more than that. By now, he was really able to live with this group of young people.

Here he was allowed to be himself completely, here he did not have to pretend, here he could be understood and here he no longer felt inferior.

Often very beautiful and unexpectedly deep conversations arose between Kevin and the others.

He could feel what was going on inside them and found the right words. They confided in him their worries and problems and to his own amazement he was usually able to help them.

With Michi he had a crazy experience.

During a conversation Kevin put his hand on Michi's shoulder and suddenly knew what the cause of his neurodermatitis was.

Little by little, something grew inside him, something he couldn't really grasp yet, but it felt good and filled him with a joyful confidence.

Maybe there was a desirable, fulfilling task for him after all and a happy future ...

On the last evening in the camp there was a strange atmosphere.

On the one hand, there was a lot of laughter and the counselors were relaxed and cheerful, but on the other hand, there was also a bit of fear and melancholy that they would soon have to master everyday life alone again.

Of course, they had already exchanged their addresses and telephone numbers with each other, so that they could stay in contact.

In addition, they all wanted to be there again at the next camp and meet there.

The campfire crackled, they grilled sausages on wooden skewers and ate potato salad.

It was a balmy summer evening, and the air was thick with smoke and goodbyes.

As always, Serena sat next to Kevin.

Especially the teams of two from the first day were now connected by a deep friendship.

Perhaps this was because they formed a kind of symbiosis with each other, that one could compensate for the weakness of the other and that together they somehow formed a whole.

He felt the same way about Serena. In a way, she was his eyes and he was her legs. So he could see and she could walk.

But there was more ...

He had fallen head over heels in love with this delicate girl, who had infected him with her optimism and joy of life. With her by his side, he was just happy.

After dinner, Serena put her hand on Kevin's hand and whispered in his ear:

"I would so love to go again to that place by the creek with you where we took a break the first day. Will you take me?"

He nodded and a pleasant shiver ran through his body.

As if it were a matter of course, he lifted Serena on his shoulders and went the way she directed him.

Even from a distance he could hear the lapping of the water and the soft rustling of the leaves of the old willow.

It smelled like damp earth and cool moss and ... it smelled like Serena, the best smell he could imagine.

Gently, he let Serena slide onto the bench by the water. For quite a while they just sat quietly next to each other, enjoying each other's company.

Once, again Kevin wondered why he couldn't hear Serena's heart ...

Their fingers touched lightly. Everything inside him began to tingle. He felt her breath very close to his face. His heart was pounding.

Serena took his hand and put it on her heart.

And there he FELT it!

Serena's heart was beating in exactly the same rhythm as his own!

Now he knew why he had never been able to hear it!

"Serena, ... I ...", Kevin tried to find the right words for his feelings.

"Yes, I know ...", Serena whispered. "I feel the same way ..." Then her lips found his.

In that moment, their two souls melted together, time seemed to stand still for a moment, and crystal clear clarity illuminated Kevin's mind.

He loved Serena, from a depth of his heart that he had no idea existed before.

And something else became clear to him at that moment.

He wanted to help other people, because he had found out here in the camp that he had developed a very sensitive perception due to his blindness and could see with his heart, so to speak.

He felt what they were missing and what they needed and for the first time in his life he felt his blindness not as a handicap but as a great gift.

Finally, he knew what his purpose in life was.

All of this became as clear to him during that kiss as if Serena were describing it.

Serena opened her eyes.

She could see the delicate glow of light that enveloped Kevin.

A small white feather floated in the air for a moment and finally landed gently on Serena's palm.

Happily, she looked up at the sky and smiled.

Then she gently put the feather in her pocket and snuggled up to Kevin.

Fire Circle

Come you guardians of the ancient knowledge,
the earth power and the creation.

Join me in the circle by the fire.

Let us experience together the element
of the highest vibration and absorb its power,
energy and passion.

Let us feel the oneness of perfection
and transform in the infinity of the divine
everything that is now allowed to go,
so that it can return in new light
and in changed form
for the highest good of all.

Let us let our spirit and soul be inspired
by the healing energy of the full moon.

Fire circle

The drums beat to the steady rhythm of the songs we sing, lifting us to the highest vibration.

We sit cross-legged around the great fire, holding hands as a symbol of connectedness.

We are all healers, wise men and guardians of the ancient knowledge whispered to us by the Great Spirit, the ancestors and the nature beings.

We are fire, water, air and earth.

We are "THE FIRE CIRCLE"....

***

Sounds slowly reach my ears as if from a dense fog.

A woodpecker is knocking somewhere on a tree in search of insects.

I turn onto my side, kick my feet free and wedge the bedspread between my knees.

Although I still have my eyelids closed, I can perceive the orange light.

Blinking cautiously, I open my eyes.

I love this moment of waking up in the morning. The moment when dream and reality mix together.

It is still very early and the first rays of sunlight are making their way through the large, open panorama window, which offers a view of the breathtaking nature.

I see the colorful meadows, through which the clear stream meanders, the forest in its deep green, and in the background the silver-grey mountains, on which there is even snow in places.

The wind plays with the light curtains and blows in the sounds and smells of the morning.

I enjoy the picture that presents itself to me, because it reflects exactly what is important to me in life: openness, security, lightness, movement, light, warmth, love and trust, as well as curiosity and freedom.

My gaze falls on my husband, who lies next to me and is still asleep.

I look at him lovingly.

The tousled hair, the beard stubble, the slight twitch around his mouth, the worry lines and the laugh lines that tell his story, of which I myself am such a big part.

We have been a couple since our youth and our relationship is something very special.

I like to compare it to the image of two trees growing next to each other and then wrapping around each other as if in an embrace. Each tree is independent, with its roots firmly anchored in the earth, and yet the trunks support each other. The branches are interwoven and form a common, protective crown, yet different leaves and fruit grow on each tree.

It's not that we always agree, not at all, but we don't want to waste valuable time wondering who is right. Rather, we try to focus on our common goals, and so we always find each other again quickly, even after an argument.

Smiling, I watch my husband.

He, too, has found his new fulfillment here. He loves to drive the quad or the tractor around the property and look after things, or to pursue his craft and creative talents in the large workshop.

I quietly climb out of bed, grab my favorite old oversized cardigan, and walk barefoot down the wooden stairs into the kitchen, where the large, cozy wooden table with its various chairs stands.

I turn on the espresso machine for my husband and brew myself a delicious tea from the herbs we dried ourselves from our garden.

On my favorite cup it says "My wishes come true" and "Just BE".

With tea in hand, I walk past the open fireplace and the large, comfortable sofa.

I open the sliding glass door to the light-flooded studio and look at the large picture I painted the day before with acrylic paints.

There are already several easels, canvases, paints and brushes in the room, just waiting for a new work of art to emerge.

I go back to the checkroom, slip into a pair of thick, self-knitted socks and step outside onto the large, covered wooden veranda.

I set the mug on the small table, which also holds my notebook and sketchpad for my next book and a few pens.

The morning sun is just dissolving the last veils of fog.

Because it's still quite cool, I wrap myself with pleasure in the thick woolen blanket before making myself comfortable in my beloved red hanging bench.

I clasp the warm cup with both hands and concentrate on the sounds around me:

The peaceful chewing and snorting of the horses, the chirping of the birds, the buzzing of the insects, the babbling of the small stream, and the regular squeaking of the chains that attach the hanging bench to the wooden beams of the porch.

A fresh, crisp breeze blows into my face and I breathe deeply into my lungs the scent of a mixture of wood, earth, grass, herbs, flowers, snow, trees, spring water and horses.

I feel alive, at rest within myself and completely in the HERE AND NOW.

Once again, I am overcome by this indescribable feeling of absolute happiness and deep gratitude.

My gaze and my thoughts wander around the grounds.

The small herd of horses stands peacefully together at the feeding trough. These dear souls have found their way to me in different ways.

Little Uncle, a white pony with black spots, came to me through the animal protection. He was found neglected and malnourished in a remote shed and was in desperate need of a new, loving home.

Djarfur, an Icelandic, was destined for the slaughterhouse because he was too big for breeding.

The eight-year-old Aramis, a beautiful Friesian black horse with tendon damage, was given to me as a side horse.

Cindy, the sweet bay Arabian mare, needed help and a loving heart, because her owner had unfortunately passed away unexpectedly.

And there was my soul horse: Luisa Dakota, a beautiful Criollo check mare. I had discovered her on the Internet, and it had been love at first sight.

At that very moment Luisa lifts her head and looks at me knowingly with her gentle brown eyes. I get goose bumps, so intense and trusting is our connection.

Ever since I can remember, horses have accompanied me in my life. I feel magically drawn to them. They are my source of energy, teachers, confidants and faithful companions.

The horses support me in my coaching seminars as co-trainers.

They open the hearts and reflect sensitively and honestly what is going on in the people.

Every time I am deeply impressed by this magical connection between human and horse and by the deep insights that are gained.

It fulfills me so much to be able to work and help the world in this way.

With pride I look at the cute and lovingly designed guest log cabins, which are arranged in a semicircle around the paddock.

Each one has its own individual touch and is comfortably furnished.

Flower hanging baskets decorate the small verandas, each with a rocking chair.

Old horseshoes with wise sayings hang above the doors.

Hammocks dangle in the wind in the trees on the grounds, and behind the cottages a barefoot path winds through the beautifully landscaped meditation garden, which is lined with fragrant flower and herb beds.

Small squares with sculptures made of wood, stone and metal as well as romantic seating areas invite you to linger and dream.

Here you can meditate, do yoga, write, or just let your mind wander and give your thoughts space in silence.

I am happy to have created a space of encounter, personal growth and mindfulness for people with this place.

It is exciting every time, hearing the stories in which people find their way here.

It doesn't matter whether they are men, women, couples or executives, most of them are people who are searching for themselves and want to develop further.

Here they can take time out from everyday life, draw new strength and energy from nature, find inner peace and clarity and get exactly the support they need.

I am already looking forward to the participants of my seminar in the coming week.

It is so much fun and joy to get to know all the different, interesting personalities, to work with them intensively and deeply, and to support them on their very own path.

I finish my tea, loll around and finally free myself from the cozy corner.

Still a bit sleepy, my husband joins me in his pajamas with a cup of cappuccino.

He gives me a kiss, puts his arm around me and together we enjoy the moment a bit more.

Today our children are coming to visit with their families, and we are looking forward to having them all around us again.

The grandchildren will be very surprised when they discover the swimming pond that my husband has built right next to the house, so that you can jump in from the porch.

The homemade elderberry lemonade they love so much is already in the fridge and I'm about to bake another delicious cake.

Before we go back into the house, I direct my gaze once again to the round square in front of the cabins.

It is the heart of this be-special place.

I put my hand on my heart and connect with the energy of the FIRE CIRCLE ...

***

Mandy's gentle voice brings us back to the present.

"Notice again the sounds and the smells and go fully into the feeling you have right now. Where can you feel it most strongly in your body? Where can it anchor? Maybe you want to put your hand on the spot. Then take another deep breath in and out and take this feeling with you before you travel back on the timeline to to-day. Move your fingers, your toes, your whole body. When you are ready, open your eyes. Welcome back to the here and now."

Wow! What a beautiful thought journey to my vision!

We lie on our mats on the floor and stretch and stretch.

Some are yawning, some are sitting up and others are staying down for a bit.

I look at the happy and relaxed faces around me and also discover my own in the large mirrored wall in front of me.

"Now take a few more minutes," Mandy continued.

"Think about what your vision is trying to tell you, what the essence of it is. Feel free to write your thoughts about it on the pad lying next to you. The important thing now is to lovingly let go of your detailed vision.

Because it is not about the fact that it has to come exactly as you have seen it now, but about the fact that the essence of it may develop and express itself.

What of it are you perhaps already living?
In which form?
Where are you allowed to show yourself more?
Where do you feel drawn to?
Which red thread runs through your life?
How can your essence express itself right now?

The universe wants you to live your essence. Your antennas are now tuned to "receive" and your subconscious mind will support you so that it comes out like that, or even much better than you can even imagine right now. Just be open to all that now wants to come to you in the next time and follow your intuition."

I reflect for a moment and realize that I am already living the essence from my vision today and that it expresses itself in many small and bigger things.

It is not HOW I bring my Soul-Heart into the world that matters, but THAT I DO.

My hands go to the places of my body where I felt that deep and strong feeling of "I-ness" again: To my heart and sacral chakra.

A memory floods me and fills every single cell of my body with the sounds of the drums beating in the steady rhythm of the songs we sing …

We hold hands and sit in a circle around the fire …

I feel the heat and the pure, powerful energy that envelops us …

***

I remember.
I remember WHO I am.
I remember WHY I am.
I remember MY PURPOSE here on earth.
I am a healer, a guardian and a bringer of light.
I remember.
I remember … THE CIRCLE OF FIRE …

I'm glad you took the time to read my stories.

I hope I was able to touch your heart and give you some beautiful moments.

If you liked it, please recommend it to others so that my stories reach many people around the world.

From the depth of my heart

Monika Staudacher

Picture credits

All paintings, sculptures and photos used in this book are made by Monika Staudacher herself.

Any further use by third parties of images or text is not permitted.

Room for personal thoughts

.

Zeitfracht Medien GmbH
Ferdinand-Jühlke-Straße 7
99095 Erfurt, Deutschland
produktsicherheit@kolibri360.de